Dinny's Diplodocus

Suddenly Dinny heard a deafening screech and, before she could turn to look behind, the giant pterosaur picked her up in his beak and carried her high over the ridge.

Dinny shut her eyes and yelled out at the top of her voice. Her mum and dad turned just in time to see Dinny dropped into the pterosaur's nest, in a high tree at the edge of the woods. She landed with a crunch and was horrified to find herself sitting on a nest of old bones!

Dinny did not need this reminder that the pterosaur enjoyed a mixed diet. And by the look of his nest, this one had a very healthy appetite!

By the same author
Paradise Park

Dinny's Diplodocus

ANGELA McALLISTER

RED FOX

A Red Fox Book

Published by Random House Children's Books
20 Vauxhall Bridge Road, London SW1V 2SA

A division of Random House UK Ltd
London Melbourne Sydney Auckland
Johannesburg and agencies throughout the world

First published in 1992 by The Bodley Head Children's Books

Red Fox edition 1993

Printed and bound in Great Britain by
Cox & Wyman Ltd, Reading, Berkshire

RANDOM HOUSE UK LIMITED Reg. No. 954009

ISBN 0 09 916031 5

CHAPTER ONE

Dinny Green knew everything there was to know about dinosaurs. She knew exactly how heavy a stegosaurus would feel if it sat on you. She knew how far to step aside if an archaeopteryx began to stretch out its wings, and how many teeth marks you could count if you were bitten by a triceratops.

Her bedroom walls were covered with posters and paintings of great spiny monsters. There were models of dinosaurs on every shelf, and her ceiling hung with flocks of low-flying pterosaurs.

Unfortunately, no one else in her family shared Dinny's interest. Her mum would often sigh as she tried to hoover around Dinny's fossil collection. 'I really don't know where she gets it from. I was only interested in horses when I was her age. . . .'

Dinny's mum had always dreamed of becoming a show-jumper, but when she grew up she became a bus driver instead. Dinny's dad was interested in wildlife, but not of the dinosaur variety. He was the manager of a garden centre. His dream was to find an undiscovered plant and become chairman of the local Rare Plant Society.

So when the Green family gathered one Saturday morning to choose their holiday, they all had very different ideas.

Mr Green knew exactly what *he* wanted to do. 'Let's go camping again on the Mudflat marshes,' he suggested,

'and continue our search for the lesser-spotted dullweed.'

A grunt came from Dinny. 'Tyrannosaurus,' she muttered. But nobody took any notice.

'There's no way I'm spending my holiday wading through a bog in leaky wellies again, Derek,' his wife insisted. 'Let's go to the Costa Palava. There are miles of wonderful beaches, and we could go pony trekking in the mountains.'

'Gorgosaurus,' growled Dinny, but her dad just gave her an annoyed look.

'I don't want to spend my holiday frying on a beach, Brenda, squeezed between crowds of horrible foreign teenagers with transistor radios,' he complained.

'Spinosaurids!' Dinny hissed. This discussion had been going on for two weeks and nobody had even asked her opinion. Her parents never seemed to agree on anything any more. They were always arguing.

'Diplodocus. Megalosaurus,' she chanted. The names

3

sounded like a witch's spell. And maybe on this particular morning they were, because the next moment something incredible happened, something that was to turn the Green family's lives upside down. . . .

Dinny's dad sat back and crossed his arms. 'Well, why don't we let Dinny decide?' he said.

'All right,' Mrs Green agreed. 'She can choose the holiday.'

Dinny couldn't believe her ears.

'DINOSAURS!' she cried, and disappeared into her bedroom.

Dinny's dad smiled confidently. He was absolutely sure she would choose to go camping on the marshes. Mrs Green calmly stroked her coffee cup. She was one

hundred per cent certain Dinny would choose to swim in the Spanish seas.

But Dinny had other ideas. . . .

She scrambled under her bed and pulled out four jigsaws, a lost netball shirt, thirty-seven comics, her earwig collection tin (which was mysteriously empty), three lost socks and a peanut-butter sandwich that looked as though it had been nibbled by escaping earwigs.

At last, right at the back, Dinny found what she was looking for, and emerged clutching a scrumpled holiday brochure. Running back to the kitchen, she presented it to her parents as if it was a ticket to paradise.

'We'll all go on a DINOSAUR HOLIDAY!' she announced.

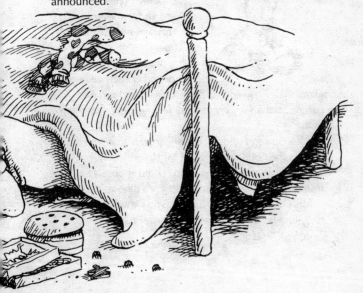

Mrs Green put on her glasses and took the grubby brochure suspiciously.

'*Dinosaur Holidays*,' she read aloud. '*Adventures among the greatest creatures that ever lived. Gasp at the Gigantosaurus; Trail the Triceratops; Track the Tyrannosaurus. Low rates out of season.*'

Dinny's smile grew wider and wider at every word. This was her dream come true.

But Mr and Mrs Green looked at each other in alarm. They considered themselves broad-minded parents, but an uncomfortable feeling crept over them both.

'Of course, I didn't actually mean that you *could* choose the holiday,' laughed Mr Green feebly.

Dinny just grinned. 'You said I could choose, Dad,' she insisted, 'and this is what I choose – a dinosaur holiday.'

Mrs Green went pale. 'Dinny, you know I'm allergic to furry things,' she said, feeling itchy already.

6

Dinny sighed impatiently. 'Mum, *everybody* knows that dinosaurs aren't furry. They are scaly, like croco-diles.'

Mr Green shuddered. A look of panic had set on his face. 'But a holiday should be mind-improving and . . . er . . . educational, and . . . and — '

'And we couldn't possibly take Grandma!' exclaimed Mrs Green, thinking she had found the perfect excuse.

At the mention of Grandma's name, Mr Green groaned. He remembered their last holiday, camping in the Damply Wetlands. Grandma had sat on his plant specimens and then cooked his collection of globgrass in with the spinach soup. And as he remembered the tempting idea of a holiday without Grandma he started to change his mind . . .

'Of course,' he said, 'Dinny should have her say in these matters, Brenda. We must be democratic, you know.'

Mrs Green sensed that for some mysterious reason she was suddenly on the losing side.

'But dinosaurs are very BIG, Dinny. They are bigger than elephants.'

Dinny thought this obvious remark wasn't worth a reply. Didn't her mother get excited about *anything* any more? When Dinny was grown up she was going to be an explorer and be excited all the time.

Meanwhile, Mr Green peered at the photos in the brochure. In the background were some interesting ferns he'd never seen before. If I brought home a specimen of those I would definitely be made chairman of the Rare Plant Society, he thought. That decided it.

'We did promise Dinny could choose,' he said, 'and we must not go back on our word.' A wicked grin started to wriggle at the edge of his mouth. 'Of course, a holiday would not be the same without Grandma, but she's really not an animal-lover, you know, Brenda.'

With a sinking heart, Mrs Green heard the firm tone of his voice and knew it was useless to argue.

'Well, I suppose even a Stone Age hotel is better than camping on those awful marshes,' she sighed. 'I just hope the food is good and the weather is hot.'

'That's settled, then. I think you ought to break the news to Grandma,' said Mr Green, and he disappeared into the shed.

Dinny cheered. It was the happiest moment of her whole life. She sat down, she stood up, she didn't know what to do, so she raced ten laps around the garden, smiling till her face ached.

When Grandma heard she was not invited to spend another holiday with the family she was actually very pleased. 'Food never quite tastes the same when you're camping,' she muttered. Instead she booked herself a scone-filled week at Doily Tiffin's Sunshine Home where no one had even heard of globgrass.

All afternoon Dinny was so excited she thought she would explode. But by bedtime she started to feel worried that her mother expected to stay in a Stone Age hotel. Should she explain that the time of the dinosaurs was millions of years *before* the Stone Age? There would certainly be no hotels where they were going – only caves. And they were self catering. . . .

Dinny finally decided it would be a pity to spoil such a perfect day. Of course everyone would like to sleep in a cave beside a crackling fire, she told herself. And so, smiling, she drifted into a dinosaur dream. . . .

9

FUSTIBARS FOSSILS

CHAPTER TWO

When Dinny woke up next morning she picked up her lucky fossil from the bedside table and shut her eyes tight.

'Please, please, please, stegosaurus knees, let it be true!' she chanted.

Sure enough, downstairs she found her father filling in the booking form at the back of the dinosaur brochure.

'This doesn't say much about accomodation, Dinny,' he muttered. 'Your mother will want a nice bathroom, you know.'

Dinny decided she suddenly had something urgent to do and disappeared before she had to answer any awkward questions.

That morning Dinny decided to walk the long route to school. This took her past a dingy, run-down old shop called Fustibar's Fossils.

The window of Fustibar's Fossils was always so dusty with cobwebs it was difficult to see the old bones and pieces of rock inside. Only someone who knew his tibula from his fibula would bother to stop and peer through the smudgy glass.

But for Dinny, Fustibar's shop was a treasure cave. The first surprise was to find that the tiny shop was actually a great cavern inside. Fat candles lit hundreds of shelves rising up the walls, crammed with ancient bones and fossil rocks. The floor was crowded with bigger bones and huge dinosaur eggs, some of them larger than Dinny herself.

Mr Fustibar was a small man, often difficult to find. He was easily hidden by a sauropod's thigh-bone, and his pale dappled suit camouflaged him among the rocks.

Mr Fustibar was always pleased to see Dinny. She was the only customer who asked interesting questions. '. . . And that is a sign of an intelligent mind,' he would say.

Dinny thought Mr Fustibar was probably one hundred years old. He always looked as if he'd just woken up and climbed out of a piece of rock himself.

His blue eyes would twinkle when he talked to Dinny about the time of the dinosaurs, bringing everything to life as if he'd been there himself that very morning. He told her about the prehistoric forests, the rumbling volcanos and the crash of great dinosaurs tearing their food from the trees. He imitated the call of flying pterosaurs, and described the plesiosaurs that swam with their long periscope necks sticking out of the water.

'*Some* people believe the Loch Ness Monster is an old plesiosaur. . . .' he once said, with a mysterious smile.

'I'm *sure* it is,' Dinny had replied. She had copies of all the Loch Ness Monster photographs on her bedroom wall. 'One day I'm going to learn how to dive so I can go to Loch Ness and find the monster — ' Mr Fustibar would lead Dinny among

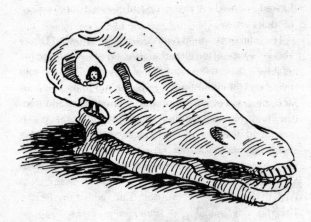

the bones to show her his treasures. Best of all
Dinny liked an enormous skull that was so big she
could stand inside it and peer out through the eye
sockets!

It had come as no surprise when one afternoon Mr
Fustibar presented her with the dinosaur holiday
brochure.

'I thought you might like this,'
he said as he parcelled up a
tyrannosaurus tooth Dinny had
been saving for. 'It's a little side-
business of mine for valued customers
and friends only.'

At the time Dinny had been so thrilled with her tooth

she hadn't taken much notice of the brochure. But when she studied it later she realized she had been offered the most exciting adventure. By hook or by crook she had been determined from that moment to have a dinosaur holiday.

And now, on this Monday morning, as Dinny gazed at Mr Fustibar's window, she enjoyed the delicious thought that her dream was about to come true. I only wish Mum and Dad weren't coming too, she sighed to herself. They're so boring these days. I'm sure they'll argue all the time. Anyway, at least there won't be a single clump of globgrass or a pony to be seen. . . .

That morning Dinny didn't have time to see Mr Fustibar because she was nearly late for school.

As she ran through the school gates she had the bad luck to meet Baz and Gordon, the school bullies.

Dinny was not only the shortest girl at Pump Lane Juniors, but the skinniest too, so she always got the full works from the boys.

'We know where you've been, Dinky Green,' sneered Baz.

'She's been at the shoe shop buying high heels!' laughed Gordon.

'No, no . . .' Baz made a snorting sort of sneer, 'Skinny Dinny's been at the fish shop trying to buy muscles!!'

Dinny gave them her fiercest scowl. 'Titanosaurus!' she barked, and as the boys laughed she pushed her way past them into school.

Dinny's only escape was in her daydreams. There she was a tyrannosaurus waiting for Baz at the school gate. As he shuffled round the corner, with his hands in his pockets, she would step out from behind the wall, swaying her great head and gnashing her teeth.

Then she would roar, 'AAARGH! . . .
BAZ FISHLIPS, YOU
ARE A SQUIRMY, SCRAWNY
LITTLE SQUIRT . . . AAARGH!'
and he would tremble,
go white as milk
and then faint in a
horrible heap.

But she was usually woken from her daydream victory by a missile from Gordon's peashooter. . . .

Poor Dinny! Every night, before she went to bed, she checked her height on a wall-chart. Then she lifted a pile of heavy books twenty times, trying to beef up her muscles. Progress was slow. But each time she felt like giving up she heard Baz's sneery snotty snort in her ears and carried on with determination.

However, Dinny did have one friend who understood how she felt and that was Miss Bean.

Miss Bean was the tallest teacher in the school. She was so tall she could change light bulbs without standing on a chair. Her nickname was Batty Bean because she was always doing unusual things. One day she decided to have a String Festival and decorated the whole school with string and rope. At the festival there were knot-tying competitions, cat's cradles, tug o' war, and everyone had to wear a string

Another time her class had a yellow day. They all wore yellow, did yellow paintings, made their own yellow lunch and wrote poems about yellow.

Everybody wanted to be in Miss Bean's class. Her face wrinkled in a kind, smiling way and she always smelt of something delicious.

One day when Dinny was helping Miss Bean to clean out the school terrapin tank she told her all about

Baz and his friends.

'I wish I was the same as everyone else . . .' Dinny sighed, squidging some green ooze from the tank between her fingers, '. . . then no one would tease me.'

Miss Bean listened carefully. 'Isn't it horrible to feel different,' she said, taking a handful of ooze herself. 'Do you know, Dinny, when I was eight like you I was already as tall as one of the teachers! Can you imagine? My clothes never fitted and people always stared at me.'

'But I bet you were good at netball, Miss,' said Dinny.

Miss Bean sighed. 'I didn't like sports, but they made me play because I could easily score goals. On Saturday mornings I

19

wanted to go to the Junior Archaeology Club but I had to go to netball practice instead.' She shook her head. 'I might have become an explorer if I hadn't had to go to netball practice. . . .'

Dinny imagined a newspaper headline – *MISS BEAN, THE TALLEST EXPLORER IN THE WORLD, DISCOVERS DINOSAUR BONES IN JUNGLE!* If only they could be explorers together one day!

Miss Bean held a terrapin close up to her nose and stroked its head. 'All the girls called me Stringy,' she explained to the terrapin with a laugh. ' "Good old Stringy Bean", that's what they called me. So you see, Dinny, I know how you feel.'

Poor Stringy Bean! thought Dinny. 'But how can I stop them teasing me?' she asked.

Miss Bean gently handed Dinny a tiny terrapin baby.

'You may not be able to stop them,' she said. 'But just have a close look at everyone else. No one is perfect, Dinny. Everyone has something unusual about them.

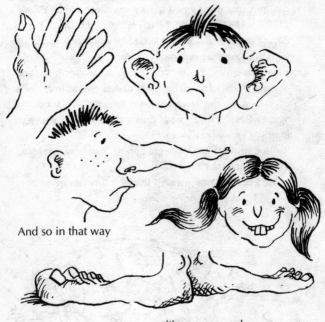

And so in that way

you *are* like everyone else.

If you are happy with what you are then bullies really cannot hurt you.' And the terrapin seemed to nod its head. 'Anyway, you might wish to be tall so much that you grow up as tall as me!'

Dinny smiled. She wouldn't mind being tall if she could be as wonderful as Miss Bean, she thought to herself. . . .

So on Monday morning when Dinny came to school full of excitement about her holiday, she went straight to Miss Bean's classroom. Miss Bean was very interested indeed and spent a long time studying the brochure.

'Oh I wish I was coming with you,' she said dreamily. 'You must draw hundreds of pictures to show me, and keep a diary every day.'

She found Dinny a big blue book with blank pages.

'I've read a few books about prehistoric times,' she explained, 'but they never sounded very real. Now you'll be able to write a true story about the dinosaurs. So don't forget your pencil!'

When Dinny got home from school that afternoon she put the blue book into her rucksack, and that was the beginning of her packing. Soon the rucksack was bulging with dinosaur reference books, a paintbox and sketch-book, her collection of baseball caps, some plaster for making casts of footprints, her best penknife, and a emergency bag of licorice.

She continued to pack and repack for four weeks and the licorice had to be replaced several times.

After what seemed like an endless wait, the holidays arrived at last.

Dinny made her final selection of vital luggage. Her mum and dad had packed exactly the same things they always packed; Mr Green had plant specimen equip-ment, indigestion tablets, socks, shorts, and a book on model aeroplanes.

Mrs Green had three bikinis, sun-tan oil, some home-work from her Spanish class, and, as a last thought, her old Girl Guide Handbook which she found in the loft.

On the morning of the holiday, Mrs Green couldn't decide whether to take a travel-sickness tablet.

'How exactly *are* we getting there, Derek?' she asked. 'You booked the holiday. Didn't you ask about trans-port?'

Mr Green couldn't remember any of the holiday details at all.

'It's a funny thing, Brenda,' he said, 'but although I talked to the booking chap, what was his name —

Fustibreath, Footsybath, Fartybrass? – although I talked to him on the phone for quite a while I don't actually remember anything he said. It's a bit weird, like a dream really. . . .'

'Oh, you're waffling as usual, Derek,' said his wife, checking the first-aid tin. 'I think we should pack our passports just in case.' And she took two travel-sickness tablets.

25

Dinny went down the road to say goodbye to Grandma, who was watching the racing on the telly.

Grandma was so delighted not to be coming that she gave Dinny five pounds pocket money for her holiday. 'Bring me back a little piece of china, ducky . . .' she said, '. . . COME ON LAZY GRAVY! COME ON BOY! ONLY ONE MORE FENCE TO GO!' Grandma shook her skinny fists at the television. 'Oh, and send me a postcard, ducks.' Then she kissed Dinny without taking her eyes off the race.

One hour later, all packed and slightly nervous, Mr and Mrs Green followed Dinny to Mr Fustibar's Fossil Shop, where they were led along a winding dusty passage to the Transportation Room.

CHAPTER THREE

The Transportation Room looked suspiciously like a junk room. It was full of boxes and broken things covered in dust, and there was one window, boarded up with cardboard.

'Now, here we are,' said Mr Fustibar, and he pulled back a curtain to reveal a large box, the size of a garden shed, made of painted wood. On the side was a wheel and some dials. The door had great brass hinges and two heavy bolts.

'It looks like the box a magician uses to make his assistant disappear,' said Mrs Green in alarm.

'And so it is, in a way,' said Mr Fustibar with a smile. 'But no one will be disappearing exactly,' he reassured her, 'just transported to another time.'

'To the land of the dinosaurs!' cried Dinny impatiently. 'Can we go now?'

'I'm not going first!' said Mrs Green.

'I'll go first,' said Dinny, already pulling back the heavy locks on the door.

'Then I'll go second,' said Mr Green.

'Oh! But I'm not going last either!' exclaimed his wife.

Mr Fustibar watched with amusement. 'You shall all go together. This box may look small but you will fit in easily, suitcases and all.'

So Dinny opened the door. The box was dark as midnight inside.

'You will find a chest of food in there and some things which may come in useful,' said Mr Fustibar. 'And you *must* remember one important thing. At this time next Saturday you must stand in the place where you arrived and I will bring you back. If you forget, I shall not be able to find you, and no one can ever get home except through this box.'

'Don't worry about that,' said Mr Green. 'We're going to spend the second week of our holiday at home, doing

the garden. I've ordered twelve new trees to be delivered on Saturday afternoon. And Dinny has to go back to school on Monday. So we shall be all packed and ready when the time comes.'

Dinny felt so excited she was ready to burst. 'Well, come on then!' she cried. 'See you next Saturday, Mr Fustibar.' And before you could say 'Muttaburrasaurus' she had disappeared into the box.

At first it was very dark inside the box. Dinny heard her parents coming in behind her.

'Oooh Derek! Hold my hand,' said her mum.

'You haven't asked me to hold your hand since we saw that horror film six years ago,' said her dad. 'Anyway, where *is* your hand, Brenda. . . .'

Suddenly a breeze of cold air made them all shiver. Then Dinny smelt a wet, weedy, pond sort of smell. From somewhere in front of them came a distant sound of gurgling water. Slowly, with her hands stretched out, Dinny walked towards the gurgling. Within a few steps a faint light appeared in the distance and as it grew stronger, Dinny found herself in a cave.

The gurgling came from a bubbling spring in a pool of clear water. Sunlight slanted into the back of the cave.

'Ah! That feels good!' sighed Dinny's mum as she stepped into the warm sunshine.

'Well, here we are then,' said Mr Green. 'I suppose this is the box of useful things.' Sure enough, there among the rocks was a tea chest labelled GREEN.

'Let's explore first,' said Dinny, shedding her rucksack. She was eager to get her first sight of a dinosaur.

'Maybe your Mr Frostybear has packed a map in here,' suggested her dad, opening the chest. First he found maps of the surrounding area, then lists of edible plants and fish and where they were to be found. There were candles and string and matches in the box, and a poster showing types of dinosaurs.

'And here is a handbook with tips on how to live in a cave and one hundred things to do in the land of the dinosaurs,' he said.

'Live in a cave!' cried Mrs Green, suddenly realizing there would be no hotel.

Dinny felt slightly responsible for her mother's mis-understanding. She took her arm and gave it a squeeze.

'Haven't you always *secretly* wanted to live in a cave, Mum? This *is* a very nice one. . . .'

Dinny's mum was shocked into silence.

'Um . . . let's explore then,' said Mr Green, who was also feeling a little guilty. And he took his wife's hand again and walked on. The cave was high and wide. There were rocky ledges like shelves jutting out of the walls, with stumps of old candles from earlier guests. Spiky stalagmites rose up from the floor and stalagtites hung from the roof.

'I bet there are good echoes in here,' said Dinny, and she took a deep breath.

'Whroop, whroop, whroop . . .' she called loudly.

'Whroop, whroop, whroop . . .' replied the echo.

'That's the sound of the parasaurolophus,' Dinny explained, showing her dad a picture of the dinosaur on their wall chart.

'I hope it's not the mating call,' laughed her father, 'or we could be in for a party!

Mrs Green had wandered to the mouth of the cave.

'Oh, come and look!' she cried, 'It's beautiful!'

Together they looked and saw that the cave was at the foot of a mountain. Stretching before them was a valley of sparkling rivers and exotic trees. Beyond that were gentle hills rising up to blue volcanoes. Birds of brilliant colours soared in the cloudless sky, and the only sound was the breeze in the trees.

'It's like paradise!' said Dinny's mum.

'Oh Brenda . . . you're going to get all poetical,' said her dad, also overcome by the sight. 'And just look at

those ferns and ginkgos.'

'What's a ginkgo, Dad?' asked Dinny, wondering why she had never heard of it. 'Is it a sort of lizard?'

'The ginkgo is the maidenhair tree,' laughed her dad. 'It has pretty leaves like fans. Ginkgos are one of the earliest trees on our planet, and yet they still grow in our park at home. We should try some gingko nuts while we're here, Brenda. They love them in Japan.'

Dinny's mum was starting to realize she wouldn't see one prawn cocktail on this holiday. Well, nuts are healthy, she told herself, gingko or otherwise.

'And now,' cried Dinny, climbing up on a rock, 'WHERE ARE THE DINOSAURS?'

Shading their eyes from the bright sun the Green family peered into the distance.

Suddenly they all saw it. A large mossy hill slowly rose up on four stumpy legs, stretched out its long neck and tail and tramped off through the trees.

'Wow!' cried Dinny. 'A giraffatitan!'

'It must be twenty-five metres long and fifteen metres high!' exclaimed her dad, sitting down on a rock in his astonishment.

'That's more than twice as long as my bus!' said her mum.

'There's another one!' cried Dinny.

'And over there!'

her dad pointed to a herd of small spiny dinosaurs basking in the sun.

Sure enough, as they looked, the forest came to life before their eyes. Long-necked dinosaurs were munching the treetops and smaller ones darted among the ferns.

'Those little ones are no bigger than chickens,' said Dinny's mum. 'I didn't realize that — '

She was interrupted by a low deep gurgling sound somewhere very close.

'Oooh! What's that?' she gasped, afraid to look around.

Dinny's dad peered cautiously about and then he whispered in her ear. 'It sounds like . . . like a tummy rumbling, Brenda,' he said nervously, 'and . . . I think it's . . . MINE! What's for lunch?'

Dinny's mum laughed with relief. 'I suppose you have the appetite of a brachiosaurus?' she smiled.

'How do you know about the brachiosaurus, Mum?' asked Dinny in surprise.

'I haven't been cleaning your room for eight years, Dinny Green, without learning a thing or two about dinosaurs,' said her mum with a wink.

CHAPTER FOUR

The Green family found a flat rock-table outside the cave and sat down to their first picnic in the land of the dinosaurs. Mr Fustibar's food chest was like a Christmas hamper full of treats. Despite her mum's disapproval, Dinny kept the binoculars firmly glued to her eyes throughout the meal.

'Well, now I want to study Mr Fustiboar's handbook,' said her dad, finding himself a comfy nook in the afternoon sun.

'And I'm going to unpack,' said her mum. 'Don't go too far, Dinny.'

But Dinny was already scrambling down the hill. With her dinosaur book in one pocket and emergency equipment in the other, she was off to find the dinosaurs. . . .

Towering conifer trees soon rose up all around and Dinny found herself in the woods. The ground was covered with moss and ferns. There were no flowers or grass at all. When she came to a clearing, Dinny found an old fallen branch. Sitting down, she took out her notebook. *My Dinosaur Book, by Dinny Green* she wrote on the first page.

From high above came the call of pterosaurs, soaring among the treetops. The warm air smelt sweet, unlike the dirty city air back home. The quietness and sunshine made Dinny feel drowsy. Home and school and Baz and Gordon seemed like a distant dream. . . .

The ferns beside her began to rustle and twitch. Out scampered a pair of strange creatures, each the size of a chicken. They were bright green, with blue snouts, long, nimble legs and spiky tails.

They didn't seem to notice Dinny as they darted about, nosing here and there for food. Dinny couldn't believe they came so close and were not afraid. She drew one in her book and put the name *Compsognathus* underneath. Then suddenly the little creatures stopped their foraging and stood very still.

Although Dinny listened hard she couldn't hear anything. But, before you could say 'disappearing dinosaurs' the compsognathuses were gone.

Dinny guessed something larger than a chicken was about to appear. She crawled among the twisted roots of a large tree, with her pencil at the ready, and waited.

Sure enough, two young diplodocuses came lolloping into the clearing. They were not much taller than Dinny herself and she knew they must be only a few weeks old.

From her hiding place, Dinny watched them play like babies, nudging and nustling each other and rolling around in the moss. Dinny had learnt all about the diplodocus when she went to the Natural History Museum with her class. She knew they only ate plants and not children. So she crawled out from the tree roots and stood quite still, offering her hand for the little dinosaurs to sniff. At first they were shy. They'd never seen a creature with a red and yellow striped body before. And where was its tail, they wondered? But as Dinny gently patted their heads they realized the stripey animal only wanted to play too. So they tickled Dinny with their noses and let her climb up on their backs and stroke their necks. Dinny named them Dip and Doc. Dip had a beautiful golden sheen on his neck and Doc had the deepest red markings on his tail. They were much brighter than the pictures in Dinny's books at home.

Dinny played with Dip and Doc all afternoon. Mr Fustibar was right – dinosaurs liked to be stroked very much. Dip and Doc rolled over again and again so that Dinny could stroke their soft yellow tummies. Dip tickled her ear with the end of his long tail, and Doc licked her nose with his rough tongue, making her giggle. Then they chased a giant dragonfly through the woods until they found a stream where the dinosaurs took a long drink.

Afterwards Dinny picked them handfuls of the tastiest fern tops. The little dinosaurs were so eager for the next mouthful they kept nudging close and toppling her into the ferns!

After a while Dinny knew she should be getting back to the cave. But first she sat on a rock to draw her new friends Dip and Doc curled up at her feet, gently waving the ends of their long tails, like contented cats.

When Dinny was finished she showed the dinosaurs their portraits, which they nibbled in approval. Then she set off towards home, hoping she might see them again another day. I can't wait to tell Miss Bean that I've actually been playing with the dinosaurs! she said to herself.

But as Dinny meandered home, she started to get a creepy feeling she was being followed. . . .

Sure enough, when she stopped she heard the thud of heavy feet on crackling twigs in the woods behind her. Dinny put her hand on the emergency parcel in her pocket, which contained a box of matches. She knew that fire would frighten unfriendly dinosaurs away, but she hoped she wouldn't have to meet a hungry tyrannosaurus. Slowly Dinny took out a match, picked up a dry twig and turned around.

All at once Dip and Doc came bounding out of the trees, knocking her over in their excitement!

'Don't you have a home to go to?' she laughed, wrestling with their great wagging tails. But the diplodocuses had decided to follow Dinny, and nothing she did could change their minds.

'Oh well!' she sighed. 'I'm sure our cave is big enough for two grown-ups and three children. I just hope you don't snore as loud as Grandma or you'll get thrown out!'

And so, as a brilliant purple and orange sunset lit up the forest, Dip and Doc followed Dinny up the hillside to the cave.

Mrs Green was gathering armfuls of fern fronds to make the beds when two heads leaned over her shoulders and munched a mouthful each!

44

She dropped the ferns in horror!

'It's all right,' laughed Dinny. 'This is Dip and Doc and they've come to stay!'

Dip and Doc thought Mrs Green must be friendly as she seemed to be waiting with supper for them. When she saw how gentle they were, Mrs Green agreed to let them stay. 'Well,' she sighed as the little dinosaurs wandered into the cave and nosed through her suitcase, 'I've never had guests who wanted to eat the beds before! What a holiday!'

So, as the sun went down Dinny curled up on her moss and fern bed between the little dinosaurs. By the light of a candle she wrote about the day's adventure. At the back of the cave her mum and dad were washing up the dishes in the spring.

'This fresh air has brought your colour back, Brenda, and the candlelight puts a sparkle in your eyes,' her dad said. 'You look just like you did on our honeymoon.'

Her mum sighed. 'It's so nice to be away from that smelly old bus garage,' she agreed. 'I must say, I really wasn't sure about Dinny's dinosaur holiday but, do you know, Derek, I'm beginning to think it might not be so bad after all. . . .'

'Good old Mr Farsterbus, or Barmyfeast or whatever he's called,' said her dad.

And smiling, sleepy Dinny agreed.

CHAPTER FIVE

The next day Dinny's mum and dad wanted to see some more dinosaurs, so the Green family went on safari. Dip and Doc gallumphed along behind, straying here and there in search of tasty branches for breakfast.

With the aid of Mr Fustibar's map, they found the steamy swamp where Mr Green was delighted to see weird trees with great swollen trunks growing out of the water. These, he explained, were great swamp cypresses.

They also found a herd of huge apatosauruses, rearing up on their hind legs to eat from the tallest treetrops. The dinosaurs peered down at Dinny and her parents for a moment, decided they weren't the sort of Greens worth eating, and carried on with their lunch.

'They must have to chew all day to fill stomachs that size,' Mr Green observed in amazement.

'Some of them don't chew at all,' Dinny explained. 'They have no teeth. They just tear off the leaves and branches and swallow them. Then they have big stones in their stomachs to grind down the food so it can be digested.'

'Maybe we should try that,' suggested her dad. 'It would save on dentist's bills.'

They soon discovered there were many dinosaurs in the swamp, most of them cleverly camouflaged.

Mrs Green spotted a stegosaurus family with six tiny babies that kept falling into the water and had to be rescued by their mother.

Dinny drew them all in her book. Mr Green collected plant specimens, and Mrs Green made everyone sun-hats from great palm leaves.

Dip and Doc paddled in the shallow swamp. They loved the juicy water plants. As it was so hot and steamy, Dinny soon waded in too. Then Mrs Green stripped off her shorts to reveal a bikini underneath and jumped in after Dinny.

'Brenda!' exclaimed Mr Green. 'You don't usually get into water unless it's frothing with your favourite bubble bath. You *do* surprise me!'

'I'm glad I can still surprise you, Derek!' laughed Mrs Green, and she lay back in the cool muddy water kicking her heels in the air.

But Mrs Green didn't expect to be surprised herself.
Dip thought his friend wanted to play. So he circled
behind her, then suddenly lifted her up on his head, high
in the air, so that she slid down his slippery neck as if it
was a water chute, and splashed into the swamp below!

Mr Green laughed so much that he lost his balance and
fell in the water too. Before you could say 'merry mud
baths' they were all sliding and splashing together.

'Who needs a hotel swimming pool when you can
have an exclusive swamp!' cried Mrs Green.

When they were all finally tired out, the Green family
trekked home. They had seen many different dinosaurs,
tall and long, fat and spiky, some with horns and frilly
collars, some with long snouts like periscopes and some

with huge sail-like fins. They had even seen some frogs and snails. Mr Green was very pleased with his growing collection of extinct plants.

Dinny and Mrs Green rode the two little dinosaurs up the hill.

'If only my old riding teacher could see me now,' chuckled Dinny's mum. 'Pony trekking will never be quite the same again. . . .'

Mr Green had become an instant swamp fanatic. 'Maybe I could dig a swamp just behind the roses in the garden?' he suggested as they washed all the mud off in the cave spring. 'I've heard mud is very good for the complexion, dear. . . .'

And so the week went by.

Mrs Green decorated their cave with paintings of dinosaurs, using crushed berries and charcoal stick. Mr Green found so many plants he had never seen before that he filled three notebooks with drawings and pressed leaves. Dinny spent sunny hours fishing with her dad and building a tree-house with her mum. Every day, with her faithful friends Dip and Doc, she explored the forests and swamps. She often wished Miss Bean could share their adventures. 'Stringy Bean would feel quite small next to all these great sauropods,' she laughed to herself. Dinny was so happy she wanted to stay in the land of the dinosaurs forever. And what made her happy more than anything else, even more than dinosaurs, was to see her mum and dad enjoying themselves together, without a cross word. This really is the perfect holiday, she thought one evening, as she watched them walk hand in hand up to the ridge to look at the sunset.

But while she watched *them*, something was watching *her*. High in the purple sky a great winged pterosaur circled slowly, its sharp eyes fixed on the tiny figure of Dinny below. While she sat on a rock dreaming, the giant bird above stretched out its sharp claws, then silently the pterosaur dipped its enormous wings and dived. The sun was too low to cast a warning shadow. Suddenly Dinny heard a deafening screech and, before she could turn to look behind, the giant pterosaur picked her up in his beak and carried her high over the ridge.

Dinny shut her eyes and yelled out at the top of her voice. Her mum and dad turned just in time to see Dinny dropped into the pterosaur's nest, in a high tree at the edge of the woods. She landed with a crunch and was horrified to find herself sitting on a nest of old bones!

Dinny did not need this reminder that the pterosaur enjoyed a mixed diet. And by the look of his nest, this one had a very healthy appetite!

She wished with all her might. 'Please, please stegosaurus knees . . . HELP!!' But nothing happened. Then nothing happened. Then nothing happened again. She opened one eye. The pterosaur was nowhere to be seen. Dinny peered up into the starry sky and just caught the silhouette of the giant bird disappearing into the night. But she know her troubles were hardly over and kept staring at the sky. For sure enough, the pterosaur would return, swooping out of the darkness, and all she could do was wait.

Mr Green woke Dip and Doc, who had been snoozing in the cave. He shouted Dinny's name frantically and pointed towards the forest. They might be too late to save Dinny unless the dinosaurs would carry them over the ridge. Dip and Doc understood that something was wrong. They let the Greens scramble on to their backs.

'This would never happen on the Costa Palava!' cried Mrs Green, hanging on to Dip's neck as they thundered towards the forest.

'Dinny will be all right,' Mr Green assured her. 'She always has a matchbox in her pocket.' He didn't mention that Dinny was wearing her pyjamas as she was carried off, and they had no pockets for emergency equipment. . . .

Meanwhile Dinny tried climbing out of the nest, but it rocked so wildly that she just had to sit very still and wait to be rescued – or eaten! As her dad guessed, she didn't have a match in her pyjamas. Her only chance

was to frighten the pter-
osaur away when it
returned. But how could
someone so small frighten
something so big? She
thought of how she was
teased for being small at
school and the memory
of Baz and Gordon made
her mad. And as she got
mad she got brave.

The sunset slipped
quickly behind the vol-
canoes. The stars came

55

out and Dinny saw shadowy winged creatures soar through the moonlight. Before long the pterosaur returned for his dinner. It circled low around the nest.

Dinny took a deep breath. 'I'm not afraid of you, Baz Fishlips!' she shouted at the top of her voice. 'I may be small,

but I'm *very* fierce.' And she made her most angry tyrannosaurus roar. 'I may be skinny but I'm *very* scary!'

The pterosaur didn't know what to make of this noisy creature. It swooped close and peered at her warily.

'I don't need to be big to be smarter than you, Baz Fishlips!' Dinny shouted even louder.

The pterosaur shied away. But it was getting very hungry.

Dinny took another deep breath, and as she paused the pterosaur's long beak zoomed towards her and gave her a prod.

Suddenly the sky lit up with flames. The pterosaur squawked in surprise and flew off sharply.

Around the tree Dinny saw her mum and dad with flaming torches. Dip and Doc, who were cowering in the shadows, came forward when they saw Dinny.

'Hold on there,' said her dad, 'Dinosaurs to the rescue!'

Then Doc stretched up his long neck and Dinny climbed out of the nest and clung to him tightly.

When Dinny was at last standing on firm ground again she rubbed her bruised knees, thanking her mum and dad.

'I sure did frighten that old pterosaur!' she laughed.

'Oh Dinny, I think we've had enough dinosaurs for one day,' said her mum as she gave her a hug.

'Except for Dip and Doc,' said Dinny gratefully.

'Except for Dip and Doc,' they all agreed.

CHAPTER SIX

At last the week drew to an end. Dinny filled the final pages of her notebook with the story of her pterosaur adventure, and Dip made a footprint on the cover. The cave with its painted walls and fern beds had become home. Mr and Mrs Green had forgotten their differences and discovered the fun of doing things together like they used to.

On Friday evening Dinny sat in the tree-house watching a herd of brachiosauruses take a mud bath, and remembering all the amazing things she had seen. Her dad climbed up beside her with a leaf full of gingko nuts to share.

'Er . . . Dinny . . .' he began, with an uncomfortable stutter, 'um . . . I have something to tell you.' Dinny was so happy she didn't hear warning bells at the tone of her father's voice. 'As you know,' he continued, 'tomorrow Mr Fistibat is expecting to transport the three of us home.'

'I wish we didn't have to go,' sighed Dinny. 'Can't we stay one more week?'

'Well, yes . . . I mean no . . . er . . . that is . . .' her father ate a handful of nuts while he tried to sort out what exactly he did mean to say. 'Well, *you* have to go back because you have school on Monday, but your mother and, um . . . your mother and I have decided to stay on an extra week. She's really enjoying herself here. Thanks to you, it's the best holiday we've ever had.'

Dinny couldn't believe her ears! 'But it was *my* idea to come here!' she protested. 'You can't stay another week without me, it's not fair!'

But Dinny's father insisted firmly that she must go back to school on Monday. 'Anyway, now that we've been once we'll be able to come again, maybe next year,' he promised.

Next year might as well be never as far as Dinny was concerned. The thought of her mum and dad enjoying the dinosaurs while she was at school was almost more than she could bear.

But her parents would not be swayed. Dinny went to

bed without any supper as a protest and lay awake most of the night trying to think of a plan.

On Saturday morning Dinny took a last walk in the forest with Dip and Doc. Then her father gave her a list of instructions.

'Now, the most important thing is to arrange with Mr Stuffyboar to transport us back at the same time next Saturday,' he said.

Mrs Green gave Dinny a letter for Grandma. Dinny was to go straight home and wait for the trees to be delivered for the garden, and then she was to go to Grandma's and stay there for the week.

As Dinny listened to all the instructions she was strangely quiet. She didn't argue at all about going home.

Her mum was puzzled by Dinny's silence, 'It's not like Dinny to give in to something so easily, Derek,' she said while Dinny was packing her rucksack. 'I expected much more trouble over this.'

'Oh I don't think there's anything to worry about,' said Mr Green. 'I think we sometimes forget how grown-up and sensible our daughter can be.'

'Hmmm. . . .' muttered Mrs Green. Her instincts told her something wasn't quite right, and Dinny's mum believed in instincts. When it was time to say goodbye, Dip and Doc were nowhere to be found. 'Well, you did say goodbye this morning,' said Dinny's mum. 'I expect they've gone back to the swamp.' Dinny looked more solemn than ever.

'I know you want to stay,' said her dad, 'but I promise we will all come back again together another time.'

'I'll look after our tree-house,' promised her mum. 'And think what fun it will be showing your notebook to everyone at school, and telling them about your holiday.'

Dinny smiled secretly. She intended to show them something much more impressive than her note-book. . . .

And so, at exactly eleven o'clock, Dinny took her last look at the land of the dinosaurs, walked through the back of the cave, and disappeared into the darkness.

For a moment, as before, Dinny found herself in complete darkness and so she stood quite still. Suddenly she heard a grunt, and a cold wet nose tickled her face. Then something nibbled her rucksack. Dip and Doc, of course, were nowhere near the swamp at all. In fact they were just about to find themselves very far from the swamp indeed.

Dinny had hidden them at the back of the cave earlier that morning, after saying a pretend goodbye in front of her parents. As Mr Fustibar was expecting to transport three people home, she thought she would give the little diplodocuses a week's holiday at her house. . . .

Mr Fustibar was very worried when Dip and Doc ambled out of the Transporter Box with Dinny. He was even more worried when her parents were nowhere to be seen.

'Oh dear!' He sat down on an ankylosaurus tail-club in astonishment. 'Dinny my dear, this won't do at all. No, no . . . this is highly irregular. This won't do at all.'

Dinny explained what had happened and how her parents wanted to extend their holiday. 'They will pay you for the extra week when they come back,' she assured him.

'Oh, that's not the problem.' Mr Fustibar shook his head and Doc nibbled his waggling ears. 'It's bad enough to have dinosaurs here, think of the trouble it will cause. But the worst part is — '

Suddenly the telephone rang in a distant office. Mr Fustibar flustered. 'Oh! What a calamity! What a disaster! I don't know what to do!'

The phone rang insistently. Throwing his hands up in despair, Mr Fustibar scuttled off to answer it.

Dinny decided it was better to leave before Mr Fustibar got more upset. She led Dip and Doc through the shop, opened the door and stepped out into the street.

Luckily the route home from Mr Fustibar's shop did not take them down the High Street. But on a Saturday morning there were plenty of people about. As everyone gasped and pointed, Dinny just looked straight ahead. Dip and Doc followed her, nibbling the tops of hedges as they went. When they passed the park, the dinosaurs stopped to tuck into a whole bed of petunias. Dinny decided to hide behind the statue until they'd finished. After all, the little dinosaurs had never tasted flowers before.

They arrived home just as the man from the garden centre drove up with his delivery of trees. Dinny hid Dip and Doc in the sitting room while the man put the potted trees all around the garden, just as Dinny instructed him. Little did he know he was making a secret hideaway for dinosaurs. . . .

CHAPTER SEVEN

By the time the tree man left, Dip and Doc had eaten all
Mrs Green's house plants, a basket of dried flowers, half
the curtains and a new dress that had been hanging by the
sewing machine. Dinny could see that feeding the hungry
dinosaurs was going to require some clever thinking. She
led them into the garden where they tucked into Mr
Green's geraniums.

'Dad can always get more plants from the garden
centre,' she thought as Dip and Doc proceeded to strip
the flowerbeds. They particularly liked the roses and Mr
Green's rare plant collection. Luckily the new trees didn't
taste so good and hid them well. So no one spotted two
baby diplodocuses that Saturday afternoon, tossing a
garden gnome between them like playful kittens.

Dinny decided to make them feel more at home by swamping up the garden a bit. She turned the garden hose on full blast and showered the little dinosaurs. They loved the water and rolled around happily on their backs. Soon the garden was very wet and muddy. She left the hose on while she made herself a triple-decker ham, jam and spam sandwich, and when she returned, the garden had become a very respectable swamp.

And so all afternoon Dip, Doc and Dinny played in the swamp. The dinosaurs had their first frozen pizzas and crisps, and they tried Coca-cola which Dinny poured into a bucket, but it gave them the sneezes.

When darkness came Dinny decided to take Dip and Doc to the park for some proper dinner.

On the way they met a lady with three poodles. When she saw them coming the lady scooped up her dogs, shouting 'Monsters, monsters! HELP!'

Poor Dip and Doc were so frightened they sat down on the pavement and refused

to move until she was out of sight.

At the park Dinny found the gingko tree her father had spoken about. Dip and Doc munched happily in the moonlight until at last they'd had enough. Then Dinny led them home, hiding from a policeman and two joggers on the way.

That night Dinny sat up at her bedroom window watching the dinosaurs asleep in the swamp-garden below. An uncomfortable feeling started to grow in her mind that two baby diplodocuses might not be an easy secret if their appetites grew any bigger. I hope the dinner ladies will have some leftovers for them, she said to herself as she drifted off to sleep. For on Monday the dinosaurs were going to school . . . .

On Monday morning Dinny was up extra early for school. As she got dressed she found her mother's note for Grandma and felt a terrible twinge of guilt. But Dinny reminded herself that Grandma didn't like pets or animals in the house. 'Anyway, I can look after myself,' she told Dip as he ate a whole box of cornflakes and twelve Weetabix for breakfast. She even polished her shoes just as her dad would have done on the first morning of term.

Dinny decided to ride Dip to school, and Doc carried her satchel around his neck. They set off early because Dinny guessed they would probably make several hedge-trimming stops along the way, and so they did. Everywhere they went people gazed in astonishment. Some thought she was from the circus or the zoo. Others thought she must be doing some sort of school project. Maybe the creatures were robots, maybe they'd been grown in the school laboratory. Maybe they were a new breed of dog, or elephants without ears. By the time Dinny and her friends arrived at the school gate they were being followed by a procession of curious people.

At the school gates all the children came out to see what the fuss was about. Someone pushed to the front of the crowd. 'Oi, move over! Get out the way!' It was Gordon making way for Baz.

'Up here, Baz!' shouted Dinny. 'Meet my friends Dip and Doc.' The two diplodocuses peered down at Baz.

69

There was a hushed silence. Everyone watched Baz, the school bully. Dip spotted a packet of chocolate in his pocket. Baz stood paralysed with fear and the crowd held their breath. Gently Dip tugged the chocolate out of Baz's pocket and ate it up, wrapper and all. Baz the bully went white as a sheet, looked up at Dinny and started to sway.

'D . . . d . . . d . . . dinosaurs!' he stuttered and fainted in a heap on the playground. The crowd cheered and

clapped their hands. Gordon suddenly felt alone and very silly. As Dip's chocolaty face loomed towards him he screamed, ran into school and locked himself in the lavatory.

Dinny laughed until she had stitches. So much for the big brave bullies. Baz and Gordon would never be able to tease her, or anyone else again after that. As the children crowded round she led the little dinosaurs into class.

This term Dinny was in

70

Class Five which was Miss Bean's class. Dinny sat the dinosaurs beside the nature table at the back of the room. The other children were shy at first, but they soon saw that Dip and Doc were not fierce at all.

'Look, they're only babies,' cried one girl and she stroked Doc's nose.

After that everyone wanted to stroke the dinosaurs. Dinny was bombarded with questions. As she took a breath to begin at the beginning Miss Bean arrived at the door. At once she saw what was happening.

'Well, well,' she exclaimed, 'I see *someone* has brought in souvenirs from her holiday!'

And so, to everyone's delight, Class Five spent the whole morning hearing the story of Dinny's dinosaur holiday.

At break-time Dip and Doc were taken up to the school field where they had a feast of grass for the first time.

When the caretaker saw the crowd on the field he came up to investigate. When he saw the dinosaurs he panicked.

'Keep away!' he shouted. 'I think we'd better evacuate the school. Don't panic, don't panic!'

But suddenly he saw how the football pitch had been miraculously trimmed. When he realized that he wouldn't have to mow the grass that afternoon he changed his mind about the two new pupils.

He decided to pretend he hadn't seen anything at all.

'All right, this is not an emergency situation,' he said, 'calm down children. Carry on, carry on.' And the children, who had been calm all the time, cheered.

However, the news that two dinosaurs were in the school soon reached the ears of Mrs Glower the headmistress. She called Miss Bean into her office.

'I have heard some extraordinary stories about one of your pupils, Miss Bean,' she began. 'I have heard that

Dinny Green rode to school on a dinosaur. I have heard that there are two *dinosaurs* on the school field. Of course I *realize* this is another of those tedious school rumours,

like the one last term about a UFO landing behind the sports hall. Of course I *know* there are no dinosaurs in the school, Miss Bean. HOWEVER, as I came out of the staffroom this morn-

ing, in my new shoes, I stepped right in a huge pile of . . . of . . .' Mrs Glower went red and flustered and broke the pencil she was holding in her hand. 'A huge pile of . . . of . . . POOH!! Miss Bean.'

Miss Bean tried to control a giggle. Mrs Glower looked at her suspiciously. 'Miss Bean, do you, or do you not, know what creature has been spending a penny outside the staffroom?'

Miss Bean truthfully replied that she didn't know what creature had spent the penny. After all, she said to herself, it could have been Dip or it could have been Doc. She really didn't know which.

Mrs Glower could see she wasn't going to get any help from Miss Bean.

73

'I'm late for a governor's lunch now,' she said, 'but when I come back I shall call up the zoo.' And Miss Bean, bursting to explode with the giggles, was dismissed.

After break Miss Bean told Dinny that the men from the zoo would be paying a visit. 'But if Dip and Doc are put in the zoo I will never be able to send them back home!' Dinny exclaimed in dismay. However, Miss Bean had an idea.

'As we have two real dinosaurs with us today,' she told the class, 'we shall spend the rest of the morning making dinosaur masks and costumes. And this afternoon we will imagine we are in the land of the dinosaurs, just as Dinny

has described to us. It will be our special project.'

And so Class Five set to work with paper and card, making tails and masks with great horns, and spikes and spines to wear on their backs. Two of the girls worked together to make a big diplodocus with a golden nose, just like Doc. They used the coloured drawings in Dinny's notebook to get their dinosaurs just right. And Dinny painted some cycad plants and huge gingko trees that reached the ceiling.

After lunch they had just finished their costumes when Mrs Glower arrived with two men in white coats from the zoo.

'I think you might find a strange creature in here,' she said as she opened the door.

The zoo men looked at the class. They saw a purple tyrannosaurus, two yellow triceratops, some stego-sauruses, an archaeopteryx with huge rainbow wings, and twenty other strange creatures. They didn't even notice two little yellow diplodocuses sitting quietly at the back.

'Yes, Mrs Glower,' said the chief zoo man. 'I can see lots of strange creatures in here. And I can also see that you need a holiday. Please don't waste our time with practical jokes like this, we've got real animals to look after.' And as Mrs Glower blushed for the second time that day, the zoo men marched out.

Poor Mrs Glower went straight to her office and rang the travel agents to book a week's holiday, then she took an aspirin and lay down quietly, for the rest of the afternoon.

CHAPTER EIGHT

Dip and Doc enjoyed their day at school. But when the last bell rang Miss Bean called Dinny aside.

'You know you can't bring the dinosaurs to school again,' she said gently. 'We managed to save them today, but it won't be long before somebody else informs the zoo. They must go back where they belong. I think you and I should go and see Mr Fustibar.'

Dinny's heart sank. But as she watched Dip and Doc hungrily nibble the paper gingko leaves, she had to agree they would be best in their own home.

So Dinny and Miss Bean set off with the little dinosaurs for Fustibar's Fossil Shop. Once they were away from school Miss Bean stopped and looked around mysteriously.

'Dinny, you did say that your mother rode one of the dinosaurs, didn't you?' she asked shyly. With a big grin Dinny guessed what Miss Bean was going to ask next.

'They are very strong, Miss,' she said. 'You could ride one easily.' Miss Bean was delighted. So she clambered up and they tramped through the side streets together. As they went, Miss Bean pretended they were explorers travelling through a secret jungle.

'Watch out for the guardians of the Water Temple!' she said as they passed the swimming baths with their dolphin statues. 'There are the red mountains of Tile City,' she cried, pointing to some far jutting roof-tops.

But when the brave explorers turned the corner into Fustibar's street, Dinny gasped in horror. The window of the fossil shop was boarded up and there was a 'For Sale' notice pasted over the door.

Dinny climbed down and tried to peer inside but there was nothing to see. The door was locked fast and she

couldn't budge it. In a
flash she remembered
how upset Mr Fustibar
had been that her par-
ents had not come home
on time. He must have
known the shop was
going to be sold. Of
course! She had sneaked
off with Dip and Doc be-
fore he had had time to tell her.

Dinny remembered the win-
dow of the Transporter Room
boarded up with cardboard. 'Let's
have a look inside,' she suggested and
led Miss Bean around the building. As Dinny had expected, the glass in the window was broken and they
easily pushed through the cardboard. They climbed
inside. The Transporter Machine stood just as Dinny
remembered it. She led Miss Bean into the shop where
everything was exactly as it had been before. The candles
were unlit and the great bones and fossils looked eerie
in the dim light from the window. But Miss Bean was
interested in everything.

'I wish you had been able to meet Mr Fustibar,' Dinny
sighed. 'He had a hundred stories about the land of the
dinosaurs.'

But Miss Bean wasn't listening. She'd been dreaming of

the great sauropods and pterosaurs as she walked among
the fossils. A wonderful idea was growing in her mind.

'Dinny, wouldn't it be exciting for the rest of the class to
learn about prehistoric times,' she said. 'As the Transporter Machine is still here we could have a class trip to the
land of the dinosaurs! If I handed out letters for the parents
tomorrow we could all go together on Thursday.'

Dinny thought it was a great idea. When she remembered the land of dinosaurs she suddenly realized that she
missed her mum and dad.

'Does that mean I get to keep Dip and Doc for a few
more days?' she asked.

'Well, I can't let you stay at home on your own.

Someone should come and look after you,' said Miss Bean. Dinny sighed and thought of Grandma. Somehow she was sure that Grandma wouldn't feel comfortable with two dinosaurs in the house. Grandma liked things neat and tidy, but a baby diplodocus did not. And then there was the little matter of the swamp. Grandma had always enjoyed the garden. . . .

Miss Bean interrupted Dinny's worried thoughts. 'I

can't see any alternative,' she said, 'I shall just have to come and stay with you myself until Thursday. That's settled then.'

And so Miss Bean fetched a suitcase from home and came to stay with Dinny and the dinosaurs. She didn't mind the swamp at all. She even drove to the park, after dark, to fetch some gingko leaves for Dip and Doc. I'm doing this for the sake of science, she said silently to herself as she crept through the park in dark glasses and an enormous coat with leaves sticking

82

out below.

The next day at school Miss Bean announced the dinosaur class trip and gave out letters for the parents. Dinny asked for special permission to invite two people from Class Six. As it was Dinny's dinosaur holiday Miss Bean agreed. So at break time Dinny hunted out Baz and Gordon, who were still recovering from their recent embarrassment, keeping a low profile behind the bicycle shed.

Baz looked very sheepish when he saw Dinny. 'I suppose you have come to have another laugh at us, eh?' he scowled.

'How were we to know those dinosaurs were only babies?' Gordon mumbled.

Dinny tried very hard not to smile. 'I haven't come to

laugh at you,' she promised. 'I've come to invite you on our class trip to the land of the dinosaurs. I've come to make friends.'

Baz still looked suspicious. 'Why are you being so nice to us?' he asked.

'*Small* people can be nice you know,' said Dinny.

Baz the ex-bully stared awkwardly at his feet.

'Come and have a look at the *big* dinosaurs,' Dinny insisted. 'They make everybody feel small!'

Baz gave a shruggy sort of smile. 'Well, all right,' he said. 'We're sorry about, you know, about teasing you. You're OK really.' And Gordon nodded his head in agreement.

And so they all agreed to be friends. Baz and Gordon had felt too foolish to ask about the dinosaurs before, but they really wanted to know all about Dinny's holiday. So she told them everything, except the part where she pretended the pterosaur was Baz!

Everyone in Dinny's class got permission to go on the trip and for two days Class Five had dinosaur fever!

On Thursday morning Miss Bean drove to school early to 'organize some things'.

The little dinosaurs sensed that something exciting was going to happen and were more frisky than usual. They took the long route to school, but when they got to Mr Fustibar's shop they found themselves following a huge lorry that parked in the middle of the street leaving no room to pass. As Dinny watched, two big men got out and

started to unlock the door of the fossil shop. Dinny suddenly realized what was happening. The lorry was a removal van and it had come to take Mr Fustibar's things away!

85

What could she do? If the Transporter Machine was taken away, Dinny could never return the dinosaurs to their own time. Worst of all, she could never bring her parents back!

She hurriedly led the dinosaurs to the back of the shop and climbed through the broken window. The men were rummaging about. They seemed to be looking for something.

'It must be 'ere somewhere,' said one gruff voice.

'I don't like pokin' about these old bones, it gives me the creeps,' said the second man. 'Anyway, I don't know what a Transposin' Machine looks like, do you 'arry?'

They were looking for the Transporter Machine! Dinny had to decide what to do fast. If she let them take the Machine, she would never see her parents again. But if she took Dip and Doc back they would all be trapped in the land of the dinosaurs forever.

Either way, her mum and dad could never come home.

Dinny thought about her friends and school, and all the things she wanted to do when she grew up. What would life be like forever in the land of the dinosaurs?

Suddenly the voices sounded nearer. 'Did you notice those strange looking elephants following the van, Stan?'

It was now or never. Dinny ran through Mr Fustibar's dark office and unlocked the back door. Harry and Stan were making so much noise in their search they didn't hear two small dinosaurs being led to the Transporter Room.

Dinny opened the door of the box and pushed Dip and Doc into the darkness. Then she switched the levers on the control panel to OUTWARD PASSAGE, turned the dial to THREE PASSENGERS, flicked the TRANS-PORT BUTTON and jumped in after them.

Once more she found herself unable to move in the

darkness. She heard a distant voice say ' 'Ere, Stan, I think I've found something — ' but then there was silence. Dip and Doc shuffled close. Then suddenly the little dinosaurs smelt the sweet scent of fresh fern fronds and Dinny saw a faint light grow before them. Slowly Dinny and the dinosaurs walked forward until they found themselves in the cave.

Mrs Green was busy peeling some roots when she heard footsteps behind her and a gentle diplodocus peered over her shoulder and nibbled the peelings from her lap!

'It's Dinny!!'
Her father came hiking
over the ridge with his
rucksack of plants. They
were all so pleased to be
reunited that for a while no
one asked why Dinny had returned.

Mrs Green showed Dinny a book of berry pictures she had painted and wooden furniture she'd built for the cave. There was a table and two chairs, and some shelves for pots that Mr Green had made.

'I found red clay in the river bed,' he explained to Dinny as he showed her plates and pots and jugs which he'd baked in the fire. Together her mum and dad had drawn up a big map of the valley, showing the types of plants and trees and where all the dinosaurs lived.

Dinny had never seen her mum and dad so happy. 'It's been such a *wonderful* holiday,' said Mrs Green, 'we really don't want to go home.'

Suddenly Dinny remembered the terrible news she had to tell her parents.

As she began to explain why none of them could ever go back home they listened with horror. 'But . . . but . . . my Spanish class . . . who will take over my shift at the garage?' cried her mum, 'And . . . and . . . and . . .' she collapsed into tears, '. . . who's going to look after Grandma!'

'What about my job and the garden?' exclaimed her dad. 'I've collected all these specimens for the Rare Plants Society. They would have made me chairman. . . .' He hung his head in his hands. Dinny tried to think of something cheerful to say.

'We'll be like the first Stone Age people,' she said. 'It will be an adventure!' But as she thought of all the things she would never see or do again her courageous smile faded. 'I wish I'd brought my skateboard,' she sighed.

'Fern salad forever!' groaned her mum.

'No telly, not even a radio, for the rest of our lives!' said

Mr Green in despair.

Even Dip rolling on his back to be tickled could not lift the spirits of the marooned Green family. As they sat together a flock of pterosaurs wheeled in the sunshine above.

The pterosaurs reminded Dinny of her new friend Baz. 'Goodbye Baz Fishlips!' she shouted as they soared overhead.

'Hello Dinky Green!' shouted Baz Fishlips.

Dinny looked up in amazement. Was she hearing voices? Sure enough, Baz stepped slowly from the cave with his eyes popping out of his head. 'Pterosaurs!' he gasped. Behind him followed Gordon, Class Five and Miss Bean, all gaping with wonder.

Dinny rubbed her eyes in astonishment. 'But some men came to take away the Transporter Machine . . .' she stammered. 'How did you get here?'

Miss Bean laughed. 'I made enquiries and found Mr Fustibar,' she explained. 'He has become the curator of a

new dinosaur museum. Next week he will collect all his fossils and bones for the museum. But he doesn't have room for the Transporter Machine any more. So I've bought it for the school. The men you saw were sent by *me* to fetch the box! When they said the door was open and your satchel caught on the lock I guessed what had happened. So here we are! Mrs Glower is going to transport us all back on Sunday. But I had to promise we wouldn't bring any dinosaurs back!'

'Well, I'd better peel some more roots for dinner, then!' said Mrs Green with great relief.

'Now you will be able to travel to the land of the dinosaurs whenever you like, Dinny,' Miss Bean promised.

'Maybe we could even bring Grandma next time!' suggested Mr Green with a wink to his wife.

Dinny grinned happily. This was probably the second best day of her life, she thought. And if she could predict the future, she would say that choosing the Green family holiday was never going to be a problem again!